A Beautiful Seashell

A Beautiful Seashell

Ruth Lercher Bornstein

Harper & Row, Publishers

A Beautiful Seashell
Copyright © 1990 by Ruth Lercher Bornstein
Printed in the U.S.A. All rights reserved.
Typography by Pat Tobin
1   2   3   4   5   6   7   8   9   10
First Edition

Library of Congress Cataloging-in-Publication Data
Bornstein, Ruth.
    A beautiful seashell / by Ruth Lercher Bornstein.
        p.   cm.
    "A Charlotte Zolotow book."
    Summary: Rosie and Great-grandmother spend a quiet time together as
Great-grandmother tells a story from her childhood in the old country.
    ISBN 0-06-020594-6. — ISBN 0-06-020595-4 (lib. bdg.)
    [1. Great-grandmothers—Fiction.]   I. Title.
PZ7.B64848Be   1990   90-4032
[E]—dc20   CIP
                                                                          AC

To Rebecca, Joseph,

Gabriel, and Jacob

Rosie and Great-Grandmother sat
in the rocking chair by the window.
They rocked and rocked.
"Grandma," said Rosie, "tell me a story.
Tell me about when you were little."
Great-Grandmother smiled.
She closed her eyes.
"When I was little," she began,

"I lived in another country,
on a hill near the sea.
At night I could hear the sea wind.
Sometimes I heard foghorns.
The sound of waves rocked me to sleep."

Rosie and Great-Grandmother
rocked and rocked.
"Tell more," said Rosie.

"One day," said Great-Grandmother,
"the foghorns called, deep and low.
My mother gave me bread and cheese
and apples in a basket, and
I climbed down the hill.

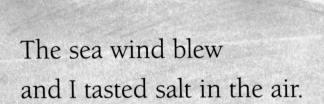

The sea wind blew
and I tasted salt in the air.

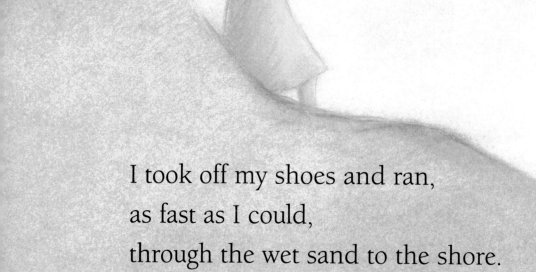

I took off my shoes and ran,
as fast as I could,
through the wet sand to the shore.

In the mist, I saw a big ship.

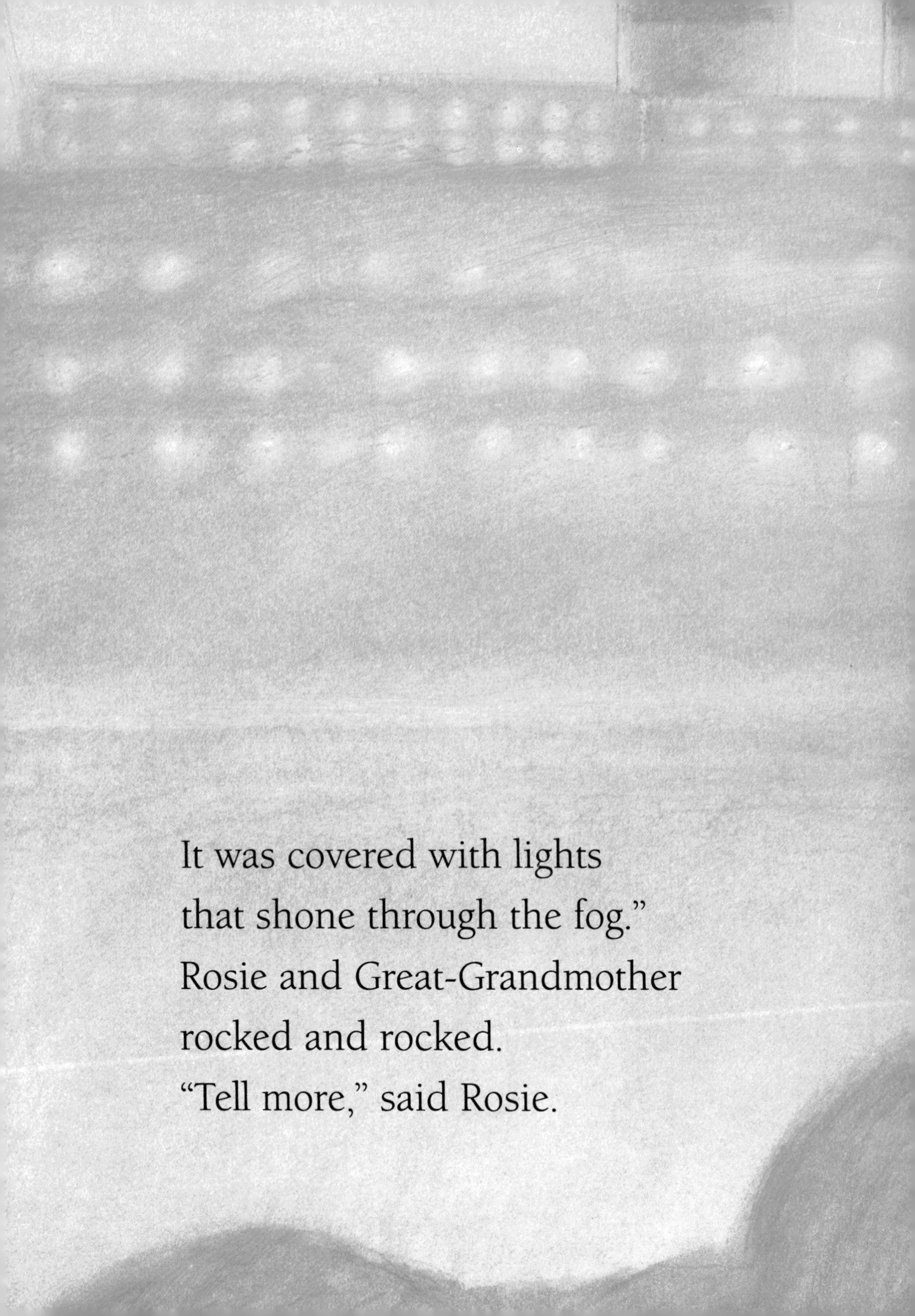

It was covered with lights
that shone through the fog."
Rosie and Great-Grandmother
rocked and rocked.
"Tell more," said Rosie.

"I watched until I couldn't see the ship anymore," said Great-Grandmother.

"Suddenly the sun broke through the fog.
The seagulls flew in from the sea.

I could almost touch them.

I whirled and twirled.
I danced in the waves.
The cold water tickled my feet.
Then my toes touched something
smooth and round under the water.
I bent down and scooped
it out of the sand."
"What was it?" asked Rosie.

"A beautiful seashell."

"Oh!" Rosie touched
Great-Grandmother's cheek.
"And then?"
Great-Grandmother opened her eyes.
She looked at Rosie.

"And then," she said, smiling,
"one day, years later,
I sailed over the waves, over the
wide sea, here to this country."
"On a big ship covered with lights?"
asked Rosie.
"Yes, on a big ship covered with lights."
Great-Grandmother reached into the
old black trunk she kept by her chair.
"This is for you," she said.

She put something in Rosie's hand.
It was smooth and round and cool.
"Your beautiful seashell!" said Rosie.
Rosie held the shell.

Then she put it to her ear.
She could hear the wind
and the sound of the waves.
She could almost hear the seagulls
and the foghorns calling.
She held the shell so
Great-Grandmother could hear.

Then Rosie and Great-Grandmother
laughed and hugged,
and rocked and rocked

and rocked.